red poppy . . . . and into a blue cornflower . . . .

Honeybee flew out of the cornflower . . . . and into . . . . .

. . . a yellow iris growing by the pond . . . .

"Hello!" quacked some ducks, "Coming for a swim?" . . . . "Sorry, I'm

". . . . . too busy," . . . . . hummed Honeybee as she disappeared into the reeds. . . . .

"Care for a fly?" croaked a friendly frog.

"No thanks," hummed Honeybee, "I'm too busy," and she flew up into a tree.

"Would you like a nut?" squeaked a squirrel. . . . . . . "No thanks, I'm too .

". . busy," hummed Honeybee . . . . . . as she flew down through the leaves. . . . . .

"Like a carrot?" asked a rabbit, popping out of his hole. . . . . "No thanks, I'm going . . .

. . back to the beehive," hummed Honeybee, and she flew over the fence. . . . .

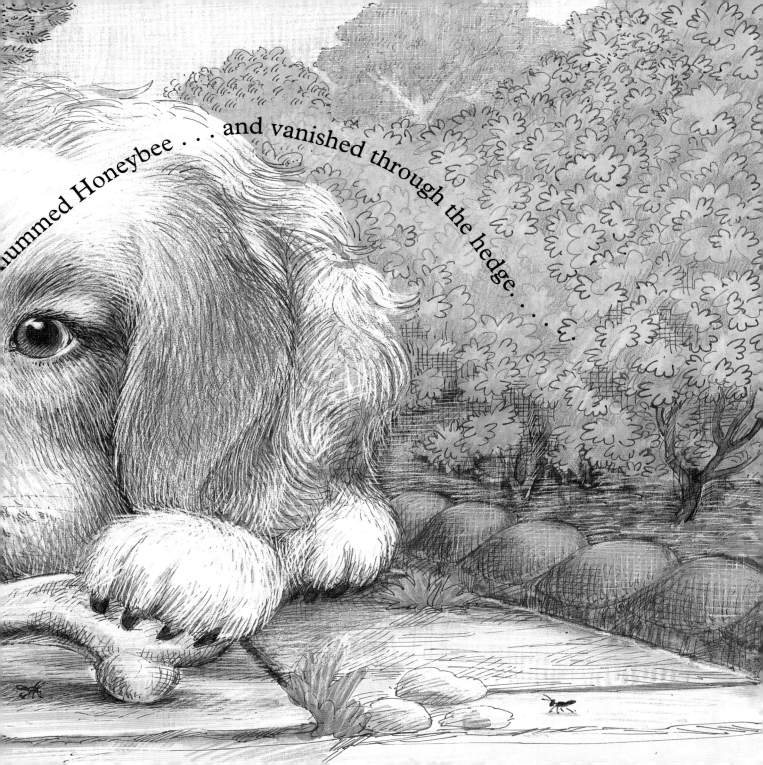

...hummed Honeybee . . . . and vanished through the hedge . . . . .

. . . . and into an orchard. . . . . . . "Hooray!" buzzed Honeybee, "There's my hive," . . .

. . . and she crawled inside . . . . . .